MORNING MYSTERY

My First Graphic Novels are published by Stone Arch Books
A Capstone Imprint
1710 Roe Crest Drive
North Mankato, Minnesota 56003
www.capstonepub.com

Library of Congress Cataloging-in-Publication data is available on the Library of Congress website.

Library Binding: 978-1-4342-1890-2
Paperback: 978-1-4342-2285-5

Summary: Brynn is having a bad morning. All sorts of things are going wrong, and she doesn't know why. Brynn needs to solve her morning mystery.

Art Director: Bob Lentz
Graphic Designer: Emily Harris
Production Specialist: Michelle Biedscheid

MORNING MYSTERY

by Christianne C. Jones

illustrated by Rémy Simard

STONE ARCH BOOKS
a capstone imprint

HOW TO READ A GRAPHIC NOVEL

Graphic novels are easy to read. Boxes called panels show you how to follow the story. Look at the panels from left to right and top to bottom.

Read the word boxes and word balloons from left to right as well. Don't forget the sound and action words in the pictures.

The pictures and the words work together to tell the whole story.

Brynn's alarm seemed extra loud on Wednesday morning.

She slowly got out of bed.

Brynn was too tired for soggy slippers.
She kicked them off.

Then she headed to the bathroom.

Brynn saw a bottle of water under her bed.

In the bathroom, Brynn grabbed the tube of toothpaste. She squeezed a little. Toothpaste went everywhere!

Brynn was not having a good day.

Brynn saw a small scissors in her bathroom.

Brynn's brother, Nolan, stopped by her room.

Brynn grabbed her backpack. She headed downstairs to the kitchen. A healthy breakfast would put her in a better mood.

Brynn grabbed the milk.

She poured it over her cereal.

The milk was green!

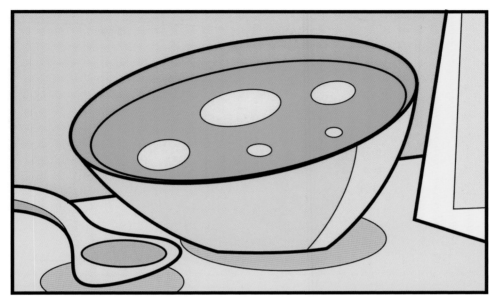

Why is the milk green?

Brynn looked around the kitchen for clues.

First she saw Nolan's green fingers.

Then she saw her mom changing the page
on the calendar.

Brynn jumped up from the table.

Brynn couldn't believe it! Her morning mystery was one big April Fools' Day joke.

Nolan started telling Brynn about his tricks.

Before Brynn woke up, Nolan had poured warm water on her slippers.

He also made cuts in her tube of toothpaste. When she squeezed it, the toothpaste shot out the sides.

The last trick was Nolan's favorite.

He added green food coloring to the milk.

Brynn was happy she had solved her morning mystery.

She couldn't wait for next year!

ABOUT THE AUTHOR

Growing up in a small town with no cable (and parents who are teachers), reading was the only thing to do. Since then, Christianne Jones has read about a bazillion books and written more than 50. Christianne works as an editor and lives in Mankato, Minnesota, with her husband (Brian) and two daughters (Lalayna and Lola).

ABOUT THE ILLUSTRATOR

Artist Rémy Simard began his career as an illustrator in 1980. Today he creates computer-generated illustrations for a large variety of clients. He has also written and illustrated more than 30 children's books in both French and English, including *Monsieur Noir et Blanc*, a finalist for Canada's Governor's Prize. To relax, Rémy likes to race around on his motorcycle. Rémy resides in Montreal with his two sons and a cat named Billy.

GLOSSARY

ALARM (uh-LARM) — an object with a buzzer or bell that wakes people up

CLUES (KLOOZ) — things that help you find the answer to a mystery

EXPLAINS (ek-SPLAYNZ) — to talk through something so it's easier to understand

MYSTERY (MISS-tur-ee) — something that is hard to understand or explain

SOGGY (SOG-ee) — very wet

DISCUSSION QUESTIONS

1. Have you ever played an April Fools' Day trick on someone? If so, what was it? If not, what would you want to do?

2. What was your favorite trick that Nolan played on Brynn? Why?

3. Do you think Nolan's tricks were funny or mean? Explain your answer.

WRITING PROMPTS

1. What kinds of tricks should Brynn play on Nolan next year? Make a list of at least three tricks she could do.

2. Brynn used clues to solve the mystery. Would you want to be a detective? Write a paragraph about your answer.

3. Were you able to solve Brynn's morning mystery? Look through the book again. List any clues you see that would help solve the mystery.

MY 1ST GRAPHIC NOVEL®

THE 1ST STEP INTO GRAPHIC NOVELS

These books are the perfect introduction to the world of safe, appealing graphic novels. Each story uses familiar topics, repeating patterns, and core vocabulary words appropriate for a beginning reader. Combine the entertaining story with comic book panels, exciting action elements, and bright colors and a safe graphic novel is born.

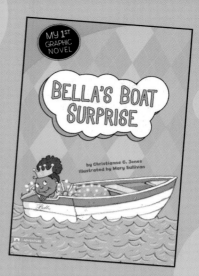